SLEEP TIGHT

SLEEP TIGHT

By

B. G. HENNESSY

Pictures by

ANTHONY CARNABUCI

A TRUMPET CLUB SPECIAL EDITION

Published by The Trumpet Club, Inc.,
a subsidiary of Bantam Doubleday Dell Publishing Group, Inc.,
1540 Broadway, New York, New York 10036.
"A Trumpet Club Special Edition" with the portrayal
of a trumpet and two circles is a registered trademark of
Bantam Doubleday Dell Publishing Group, Inc.

ISBN 0-440-83255-1

This edition published by arrangement with
Viking Penguin, a division of Penguin Books USA Inc.

Printed in the United States of America
September 1995   UPR   10 9 8 7 6 5 4 3 2 1

Set in 22 point Plantin Light.

For Brett Michael
—B.G.H.

To Patricia,
my love and inspiration
—A.C.

Night time

Quiet time

Read our favorite book time

Cozy time

Whisper time

Time to go to sleep time

Who is sleeping?

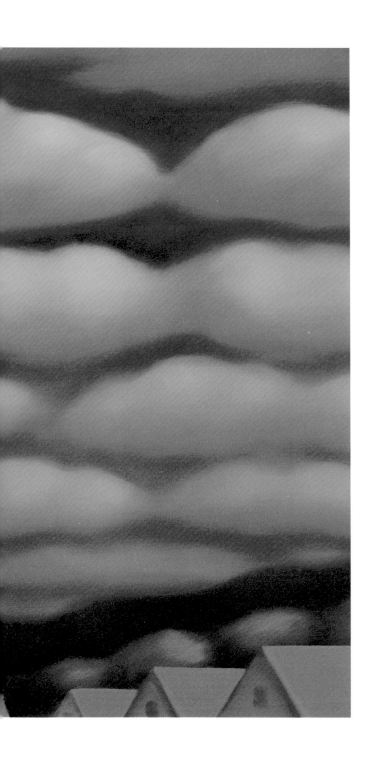

Birds are sleeping in the trees

Clouds are sleeping on a breeze

Trains are sleeping on the tracks

Bugs are sleeping in the cracks

Stores are sleeping in the town

Grass is sleeping on the ground

Birds, clouds, trains, trees

Bugs, cracks, stores, breeze

Grass, town, tracks, ground

Things are sleeping all around

Who is sleeping in our room?

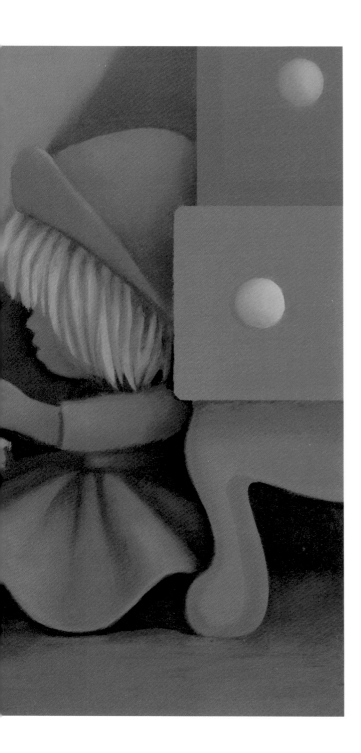

Our socks are sleeping in a drawer

Our shoes are sleeping on the floor

Our soap is sleeping in the tub

Our blocks are sleeping on the rug

Our books are sleeping on a chair

Rabbit's sleeping next to bear

Shoes, chair, soap, blocks

Books, bear, tub, socks

Pillow, blanket, bed, night-light

A song, a yawn, then sleep tight.